Paw Prints

Siberian Huskies

by Nadia Higgins

Bullfrog
Books

Ideas for Parents and Teachers

Bullfrog Books let children practice reading informational text at the earliest reading levels. Repetition, familiar words, and photo labels support early readers.

Before Reading

- Discuss the cover photo. What does it tell them?
- Look at the picture glossary together. Read and discuss the words.

Read the Book

- "Walk" through the book and look at the photos. Let the child ask questions. Point out the photo labels.
- Read the book to the child, or have him or her read independently.

After Reading

- Prompt the child to think more. Ask: Have you ever been pulled by a sled dog? Would you want to be?

Bullfrog Books are published by Jump!
5357 Penn Avenue South
Minneapolis, MN 55419
www.jumplibrary.com

Copyright © 2019 Jump! International copyright reserved in all countries. No part of this book may be reproduced in any form without written permission from the publisher.

Library of Congress Cataloging-in-Publication Data

Names: Higgins, Nadia, author.
Title: Siberian huskies / by Nadia Higgins.
Description: Minneapolis, MN : Jump!, Inc., 2018.
Series: Paw prints | Series: Bullfrog books
Includes index.
Audience: Ages 5 to 8. | Audience: Grades K to 3.
Identifiers: LCCN 2017044077 (print)
LCCN 2017044361 (ebook)
ISBN 9781624967870 (ebook)
ISBN 9781624967863 (hardcover : alk. paper)
Subjects: LCSH: Siberian husky—Juvenile literature.
Classification: LCC SF429.S65 (ebook)
LCC SF429.S65 H54 2018 (print) | DDC 636.73—dc23
LC record available at https://lccn.loc.gov/2017044077

Editor: Jenna Trnka
Book Designer: Molly Ballanger

Photo Credits: GlobalP/iStock, cover; Dora Zett/Shutterstock, 1, 16; Dmitry Kalinovsky/Shutterstock, 3; SVPhilon/Shutterstock, 4, 23bl; Chirtsova Natalia/Shutterstock, 5; Stephen Moehle/Shutterstock, 6–7; Alaska Stock Images/Age Fotostock, 8–9, 23tl; Zero Creatives/Getty, 10–11; otsphoto/Shutterstock, 12; Yato Kenshin/Shutterstock, 13; SashaS Skvortcova/Shutterstock, 14–15, 23br; artisteer/iStock, 17; madcorona/iStock, 18–19, 23tr; Lane Oatey/Blue Jean Images/Getty, 20–21 (foreground); Laura Gunn/Shutterstock, 20–21 (background); Nataliya Sdobnikova/Shutterstock, 22; Dan Kosmayer/Shutterstock, 24.

Printed in the United States of America at Corporate Graphics in North Mankato, Minnesota.

Table of Contents

Furry and Friendly 4

A Siberian Husky Up Close 22

Picture Glossary 23

Index 24

To Learn More 24

Furry and Friendly

A Siberian husky looks like a wolf.

But it is a furry, friendly dog.

5

These dogs are nice.
They wag their tails!

sled

These dogs were
bred in Asia.

They were sled dogs.

They still love to run.

They still love to pull.

Huskies love snow.

They do not get cold.

13

fur

Their fur has two layers.
The bottom is soft.
The top is coarse.

Huskies come in many colors.
Black, white, red, and brown.

Most have icy blue eyes.

17

Arrooooooo!

These dogs sure can howl.

What does she want?

More attention, please!

A Siberian Husky Up Close

ear

tail

coat

paw

Picture Glossary

bred
Developed as
a dog breed.

howl
To make a long,
loud sound.

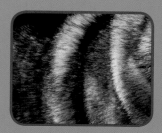

coarse
Thick and wiry.

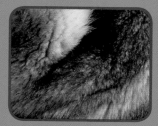

layers
Coatings of
something.

Index

Asia 9

colors 16

eyes 17

friendly 5

fur 15

howl 18

pull 10

run 10

sled dogs 9

snow 12

tails 6

wolf 4

To Learn More

Learning more is as easy as 1, 2, 3.

1) Go to www.factsurfer.com

2) Enter "Siberianhuskies" into the search box.

3) Click the "Surf" button to see a list of websites.

With factsurfer.com, finding more information is just a click away.